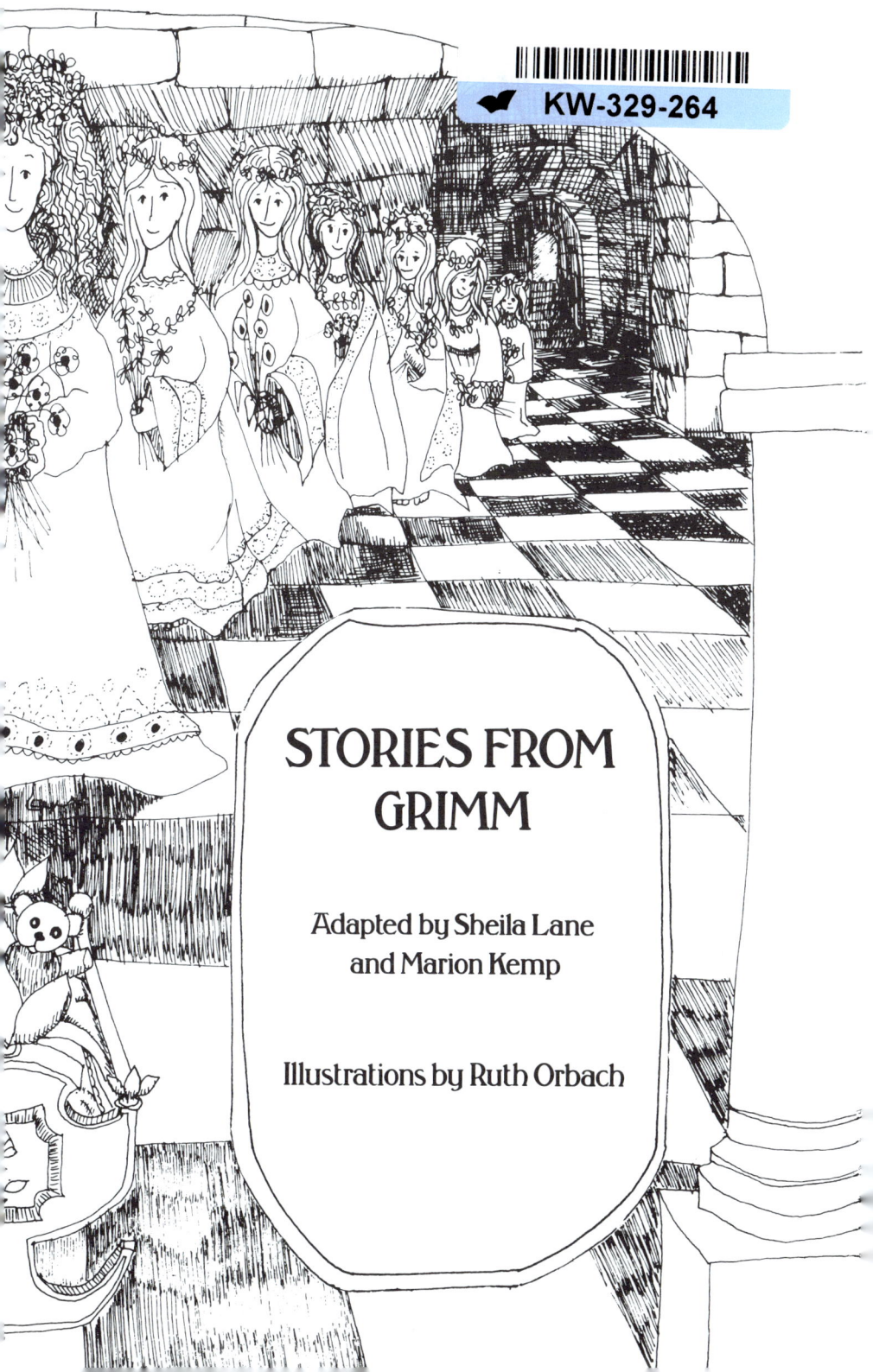

STORIES FROM GRIMM

Adapted by Sheila Lane and Marion Kemp

Illustrations by Ruth Orbach

WARD LOCK EDUCATIONAL CO., LTD.
BIC LING KEE HOUSE
1 CHRISTOPHER ROAD
EAST GRINSTEAD
SUSSEX RH19 3BT
ENGLAND

A MEMBER OF THE LING KEE GROUP
HONG KONG • SINGAPORE • LONDON • NEW YORK

This adaptation ©Shelia Lane and Marion Kemp 1978
Reprinted 1981, 1983, 1984, 1986, 1991, 1996

ISBN 0-7062-3754-4

Printed in Hong Kong

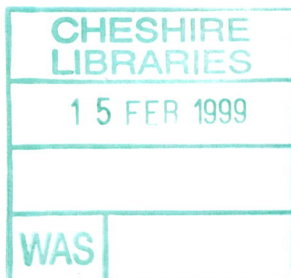

STORIES FROM GRIMM

Adapted by Sheila Lane and Marion Kemp

Illustrations by Ruth Orbach

Take Part Series
Ward Lock Educational

Contents

* This sign means that you can make the sounds which go with the story.

Hansel and Gretel

The people in the story are:

Hansel

Gretel, his sister

Wicked Witch

Once there were two children who lived with their father and stepmother at the edge of a great forest. The family became so poor that, one day, the stepmother made her husband take the children into the forest and leave them there.

Gretel   I do not like it here.

Hansel   Soon it will be morning and then we shall be able to find our way. Go to sleep for a little while, Gretel.

Gretel   But I cannot go to sleep here.

Hansel   When morning comes we will find the woodcutter's hut and wait for our father to come to his work. We don't want to go back to our stepmother again, do we?

Gretel   No! No!
I do not want to go back to our stepmother. I ... I ... I ... *
Hansel   Crying won't help us. Look! I do believe it's getting lighter..

Gretel   Do you know the way to the woodcutter's hut, Hansel?

Hansel   Well ... Yes ... Well ... I think so.

Gretel   I think we are lost. Oh! Oh! Oh! *

Hansel   Oh, Gretel, don't cry again. Look! There's the great oak tree we used to play under. We must be going the right way.

Gretel   There are a lot of oak trees in the forest.
All the oak trees look the same to me.
I do not think we are going the right way, Hansel.
I think we are lost.

Hansel   Perhaps you're right, Gretel. There *are* lots of oak trees in the forest and they *do* look the same.

Gretel   What shall we do, Hansel?
Oh, what shall we do?
We *are* lost.

8

Hansel   I know that you are tired and hungry, Gretel, but you must be brave. We must keep walking so that we can find our way to the woodcutter's hut. I know what we'll do! We'll look for some blackberries to eat.
Wait! Look! What's that?

Gretel   What can you see, Hansel?

Hansel   Look over there! I can see something through the trees.
Take my hand, Gretel. Come along.

Gretel   What is it?
What can you see through the trees?

Hansel   I think it's a house. It looks like a house. Oh Gretel! Doesn't it look lovely? It looks like a house made of cake and sweets.

Gretel   ＊It smells like cake and sweets too.

Hansel   I'm going to creep up to the window and look in …
Oh! A bit has broken off in my hand. * Smell it, Gretel.
It smells just like gingerbread cake.

Gretel   It smells good.

Hansel   I'm going to put just a little piece in my mouth.
Oh my! It *tastes* good too.

Gretel   Give me a bit.
Oh yes, it's lovely.

Hansel   I do believe the whole house is made of cakes and
sweets.
Watch me break a piece off and put it in my pocket.

Gretel   No, don't do that, Hansel.
The house might belong to someone.
Someone might come out.

Hansel   I don't care. I'm hungry. Come on! The windows taste
just like the icing on the birthday cakes our mother used to
make.

Gretel   Oh, Hansel, we are in luck.
Now we have lots of food.

Hansel   Sh! * What was that? I thought I heard someone
speak.

Wicked Witch   Tip, tap, who goes there?
Or is it the wind that blows through the air?

Gretel   It's an old lady.
She is looking out of the window.

Hansel   And I've got a piece of her window in my pocket!

Wicked Witch   Well! Well! Well!
It isn't the wind that blows through the air, but it's two little children, pretty and fair.
Ah! What dear little children, to be sure.

Hansel   Good day to you, mistress.

Gretel   Good day to you, mistress.

Wicked Witch   Good day to you, my dears. You look hungry to be sure.
Come along with me and I'll find you something good to eat.

Hansel   Oh, thank you. We've been walking in the forest for many hours and we're very tired.

Gretel   Yes, we are very tired.
Have you a bed for us to sleep in?

Wicked Witch   Yes! Yes! But first you must both have a good supper of milk and pancakes. There! Eat away! *

Hansel   Thank you, mistress. You are very kind.

Gretel   Thank you. I love milk and pancakes.

Wicked Witch   Now you must get some sleep. See, here are two little white beds. Get into them, my dears. Sleep well!

The next morning the wicked witch crept into the room where Hansel and Gretel were sleeping.

Wicked Witch   Aha! It's getting lighter. Morning has come.
Now! Where are those two sleeping beauties?
Ha! Ha! How peaceful they look.
Little do they know what is in my mind. Aha! Wake up, boy!

Hansel   Where am I? ... Who are you?

Wicked Witch   Don't you remember me, my dear?

Hansel   Oh yes, mistress. You gave us some supper last night.

Wicked Witch   Wake up, girl!
You can just get out of your bed, my dear, and sweep the floor.
Come here, boy! Let me look at you.
What bony shoulders you've got!

Hansel   Ow! Don't do that. It hurt. Ow!

Gretel   Don't do that. You're hurting him.

Wicked Witch   Aha! Little do you know who I am.

Hansel   Last night I thought you were a kind old woman. But this morning I think you're a ... wicked ... old ... WITCH!

Wicked Witch   Take that! * And that! * And that! * You rude boy!

Gretel   Don't do that. You're hurting him.

Wicked Witch   And I'll hurt you too, my girl, if that floor isn't swept and the dishes washed. Now, in there with you, my boy! *

Hansel   No! No! I'm not going in there. It looks like some sort of cage. Gretel! Gretel! It is a cage and there's a lock on the door. Stop her!

Gretel   Stop! Stop! You're a wicked old witch!

Wicked Witch   You bad girl! Take that! * And that! * And that! *

Gretel   Oh! Oh! I am going to run …

Hansel   No, Gretel! Don't leave me here. She's locked me in. Please don't leave me.

Wicked Witch   Aha! You're not going, my girl. I've got the pair of you now, one in the cage and one to work. Come along, lazy bones, go and fetch some water. I want to cook something nice for your brother. I want him fat, as fat as can be. The sooner he's fat, the sooner I can eat him for my dinner! Ha! Ha!

Hansel   No! No! No!

Gretel   You can't do that.

Wicked Witch   I'll do as I like and you'll do as I say. I'm going to cook a good thick stew full of potatoes and noodles.

Gretel   Please … do … not … eat … my … brother … Hansel. Please … do … not … eat … him. Oh! Oh! Oh! *

Wicked Witch   Stop crying, girl, and help me to cook the meal. We will cook him a big meal three times a day. He will grow fatter and fatter and when he is ready I shall have him for my dinner! Aha!

So day after day Hansel had three big meals and he grew fatter and fatter, whilst poor Gretel grew thinner and thinner.

Wicked Witch   Aha! Give me your arm, boy. Aha! Yes, you're lovely and plump now. You're as plump as a chicken ready for the oven. I'll have you today! Aha! Light the fire, girl, and put water in the pan. I'll have Hansel for my dinner today, with plenty of gravy to dip the bread in. Aha!

Gretel   No! No! Please do not eat my brother.
Please do not have him for your dinner.
I'll cook you a good meal. But please do not eat Hansel.

Wicked Witch   Be quiet, girl, and do as you are told. We'll bake the bread first. I'll make the dough while you creep into the oven and see if it is hot enough.

Hansel   Sh! Gretel! Say you don't know how to get in.

Gretel   But I don't see how to get in.
I just don't see how to get into the oven.

Wicked Witch   Stupid! Simpleton! Anyone could do it.

Hansel   Sh! Gretel! Tell her to show you how to do it.

Gretel   Then show me how to do it.

Wicked Witch   You stupid girl! All right, I'll show you. Just put your head in, like this.

Hansel   Sh! Make her go farther in, Gretel. Make her go farther in.

Gretel   Show me a bit more.
Go a bit farther in.

Wicked Witch   Like this, you simpleton! Like this!

Hansel   Give her a push!

Gretel   She's in! She's in!

Hansel   Bang the oven door. *

Gretel   She's in!
Hansel!
She's in and she cannot get out!

Hansel   Pull down the catch! Quick, Gretel! Pull down the catch!

Gretel   * I've done it!
There, I've done it!

Hansel   Hurrah! Bravo! We've shut the old witch in the oven. Now the old woman will roast in her own oven. Soon she'll be dead and serve her right! She's a wicked old witch. Let me out of this cage now, Gretel. Come and undo the latch. Be quick!

Gretel   I'm coming! *
Yes, I will undo the latch.
Come out, Hansel! Come out!

Hansel   We're free! Gretel! Gretel! We're free!
Let's dance and be merry! *

Gretel   Come on, now, Hansel.
Let's get out of here.

Hansel   Not yet. We'll look round the cottage first and see
what we can find. There's treasure in the chest. I've seen the old
witch taking it out at night and counting it.

Gretel   What kind of treasure?

Hansel   There's gold and silver and all kinds of jewels. Look!

Gretel   Oh Hansel!
The chest is full of treasure.
We are rich.

Hansel   I'll stuff my pockets with these pearls and you can fill your apron with these gold and silver pieces.

Gretel   Now our father will be rich.
How glad he will be to see us.
Come on, Hansel, let us find our way back to him.

Hansel   I'm coming, but I'll just break off a big piece of cake and a piece of sugar icing for us to eat on the way.

As if by magic Hansel and Gretel found the way back to their home at the edge of the forest. Their father was overjoyed to see them alive and well and with the treasure from the wicked witch's cottage they all lived happily ever after.

Briar Rose or Princess Rosebud

The people in the story are:

Bad Fairy

Good Fairy

King   **Queen**

Prince   **Princess Rosebud**

21

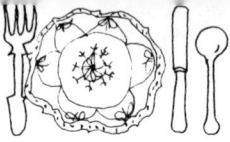

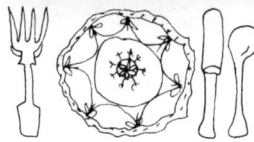

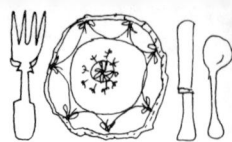

There once lived a king and queen who wished every day that they could have a child. After many years their wish was granted and a beautiful baby girl was born.

King   This is the happiest day of my life. I have never seen such a lovely child. Let me look again at her beautiful blue eyes.

Queen   Her eyes are as blue as the sky.

King   And her hair is black as a raven's wing.
We have the most beautiful child in the world, so everyone in the kingdom must be invited to come and see her. We will have a great feast for her christening.

Queen   Must we invite *everyone* to her christening?

King   Yes, my dear. The whole kingdom must be invited. We will invite not only our friends and relations, but also all the people who work in the kingdom.

Queen   But we don't know all the people who work in the kingdom.

King   No, my dear, but we will invite them because they will want to see the child. Besides, they will enjoy a great feast.

Queen   That is so.
Everyone enjoys a feast.

King   And of course, we will invite all the fairies. We will invite all the thirteen fairies of the kingdom.

Queen   Oh no, my dear.
We can't do that.

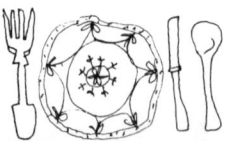

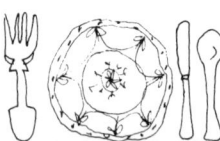

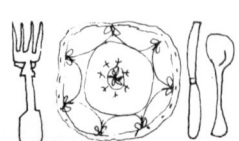

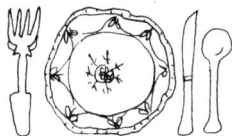

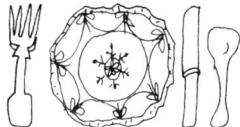

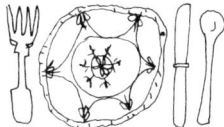

King   But why not?

Queen   Fairies must have gold plates to eat off.
A fairy cannot eat off a plate that is not made of gold.

King   But we have a set of beautiful gold plates in the palace.

Queen   How many fairies did you say?

King   Thirteen, of course. They are the thirteen fairies of the
kingdom.

Queen   And how many gold plates are there in a set?

King   Oh dear! Yes, of course. There are only twelve.

Queen   So what shall we do?

King   We shall have to leave one out,
of course. The thirteenth fairy
of this kingdom is a bad fairy
anyway. So we just won't
invite her.

Queen   She won't like that.

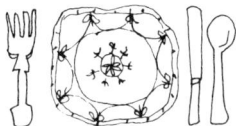

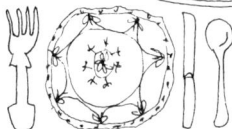

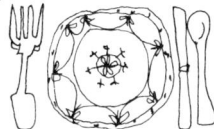

King   Don't worry, my dear. Perhaps she won't even hear about it. In any case I had planned that the twelve good fairies of the kingdom should be our child's godmothers. We really don't want the thirteenth fairy because she might bring bad luck.

Queen   We don't want our child to have bad luck. We want our child to be happy for ever.

So a splendid christening feast was held.
Soon it was time for the fairies to present their magic gifts to the child.

Good Fairy   What christian names have you chosen for the child?

King   The queen and I have read all the names in *The Great Book of Christian Names*, but there isn't one which is exactly right. We want a name which is different.

Good Fairy   The child is so beautiful as she lies there sleeping in her mother's arms. Why! She is just like a tiny rosebud.

Queen   Yes, you are right.
She *is* just like a tiny rosebud.

King   That's it! The first good fairy has chosen the name.

Good Fairy   I don't think I have. I didn't say a name at all.

King   But you said that our little princess is like a tiny ROSEBUD. That is what she shall be called. Do you like the name, my dear?

Queen   Princess Rosebud! Princess Rosebud!
Yes, that is a beautiful name for a beautiful child.

Good Fairy   So that is the first gift to our princess. I, the first good fairy, give the little princess the gift of the name Rosebud.
Now, what other gifts have my sister fairies brought?

King   Let all the fairies of the kingdom come forward and present their gifts.

Queen   And the first good fairy shall tell us what they are.

Good Fairy   Come forward, fairies.

These are the gifts:
first . . . . beauty
second. . . . . . riches
third . . . . happiness
fourth. . . . . . . kindness
fifth . . . . goodness
sixth. . . . . gentleness
seventh . . . . . truthfulness
eighth . . . . . . generosity
ninth . . . . common sense

Yes, that makes ten, counting my own gift of a name.

King   Our daughter has been given every possible gift there is in our kingdom.

Queen   No other child in the world can ever have had so many gifts.

Good Fairy   But wait! We have not finished. There is a most precious gift yet to come. Here it is! The eleventh fairy gives the princess the gift of ... intelligence.

King   Now our daughter must surely have every possible gift.

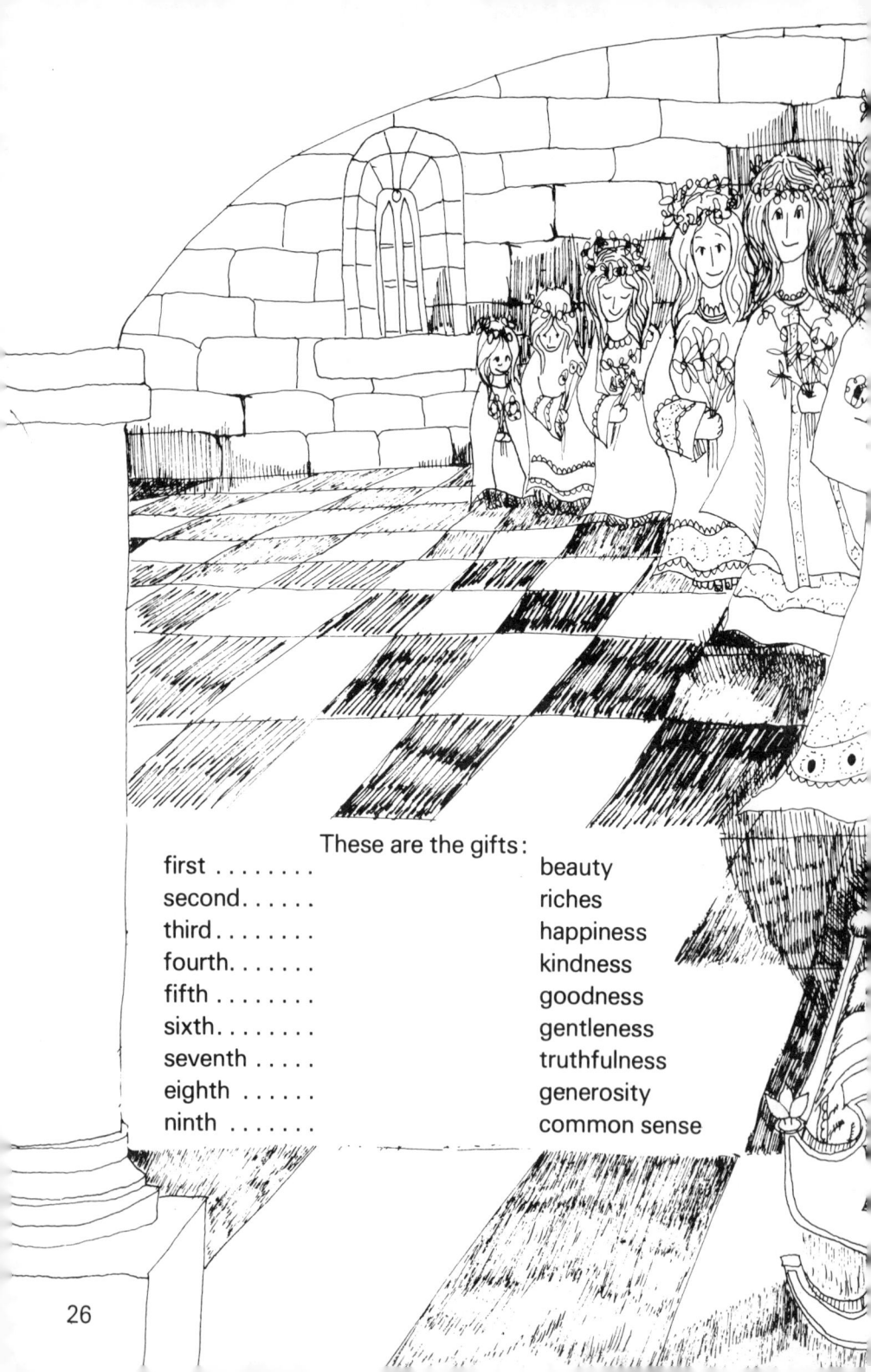

These are the gifts:

first	beauty
second	riches
third	happiness
fourth	kindness
fifth	goodness
sixth	gentleness
seventh	truthfulness
eighth	generosity
ninth	common sense

Bad Fairy   NO! NO! NO!
She has not had my gift yet.

Queen   Go away! Go away!

King   You have not been invited.

Bad Fairy   And why not?
Why didn't you invite me?
Tell me that.

Queen   We did not have a gold
plate for you.

King   That is true. The only reason for not inviting you was that
we have only twelve plates made of gold in a set. And there are
thirteen fairies in the kingdom.

Bad Fairy   Tell me why *I* was the one left out.
Tell me that.

Queen   Someone had to be left out.

King   And everyone knows that thirteen is an unlucky number.

Bad Fairy   Tell me why I had to be the unlucky one.
Tell me that.

Good Fairy   Please, dear sister, do not spoil this lovely
christening party by being so angry. Look! You can have my
plate. I have brushed the crumbs off.

Bad Fairy   I do not want your plate, sister.
There is one crumb still on it.
Why should I have your plate?
Tell me that.

Good Fairy   Oh dear. This is getting very difficult. Listen sister, all the fairies who were invited to the christening party came to be god-parents, and each one brought a gift.

Bad Fairy   Oh, but I *have* brought a gift. I told you when I came in.

King   Then we are very pleased to have it.

Queen   I hope that we shall be pleased to have it.

Good Fairy   Be careful! Oh, please be careful before you accept anything from this sister of mine.

Bad Fairy   It is not for you to say, sister.
I have a gift and I will give it.
I will tell you all what it is.

Queen   I do hope that it is something good.
I do hope that it is something we want our child to have.

Bad Fairy   No! No! No! You did not want me here.
So I will give your child a gift *she* does not want.

King   No!

Queen   No!

Good Fairy   No!

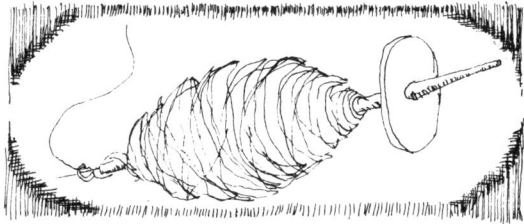

Bad Fairy   Yes! Yes! Yes! And this is it.

When your child is just fifteen years old, she will prick her finger on a S ... P ... I ... N ... D ... L ... E! Then she will fall down and ...

Good Fairy   Stop! Your gift has been made and it cannot be taken back. But there is still one more yet to come.
What is the gift of the twelfth fairy?

Bad Fairy   I do not care about the gift of the twelfth fairy.
I say that when the child is just fifteen years old, she will prick
her finger on a spindle and then she will fall ...

Good Fairy   ... ASLEEP! That is the gift of the twelfth fairy,
the gift of sleep. The child will fall asleep for a hundred years ...
but she will not die.

Queen   Oh no! Oh no!
What shall we do?
Oh! Oh!

King   Do not cry, my dear. I know just what to do. The bad
fairy said that our princess will prick her finger on a spindle. Only
the sharp point on the needle of a spindle can harm our child. I
will order that every spindle in the kingdom shall be burnt.

Queen   But will she be safe?
Perhaps she will prick her finger on something else.

Good Fairy   In that case she will not be harmed. The spell has
been given and it cannot be changed. *You* cannot change it and
the bad fairy cannot change it. So, *burn all the spindles*.

And so it was that all the spindles which could be found in the
kingdom were burnt.
Now it happened that fifteen years later, the princess Rosebud
was exploring an old tower in a part of the palace which was
never used.

Rosebud   I have never been up here before. I do love exploring
new places. I wonder where that door leads to? The key is very
old and rusty, but I think I can turn it. *
One more try and I will have the door open. *
Oh!

Bad Fairy   Good day to you, princess.
You *are* a princess, I believe.

Rosebud   Oh! Good day to you old dame.
Yes, I am the princess Rosebud.

Bad Fairy   That's a very pretty name
and you are a very pretty princess.

Rosebud   Thank you kindly, old dame.
I was given my name by the good fairy
when I was christened.

Bad Fairy   If the good fairy gave you your name, what did the
bad fairy give you? Tell me that.

Rosebud   I'm sure there were no bad fairies at my christening.
I have never been told about one.

Bad Fairy   That is all right then.

Rosebud   Now, tell me something, old dame. What are you
doing up here?

Bad Fairy   I'm spinning flax.

Rosebud   Yes, I can see that. But what sort of thing is that?
What is it that rattles round and round as you go?

Bad Fairy   Have you never seen one of these … things before,
princess Rosebud?

Rosebud   No, never. I've never seen flax spin round on a wheel
like that before. What is it called, please?

Bad Fairy   It is called a S P I N D L E!

Rosebud   That's a very good name for it, because it spins round and round.

Bad Fairy   Do you see that pin down there?

Rosebud   No, I don't think so. Ah! Is that it down by that sharp point?

Bad Fairy   What sharp point?

Rosebud   That one down there.

Bad Fairy   I can't see a sharp point. But, of course, I am a very old woman and my eyes are getting dim. Just show it to me, princess Rosebud. Put your beautiful little finger on the point.

Rosebud   There!

Bad Fairy   And THERE!

Rosebud   Oh! Oh! *

Bad Fairy   Ha! Ha! Ha! And so my gift comes true. The beautiful princess Rosebud has fallen to the floor ... not dead ... because of that good fairy ... but fast asleep for a hundred years. Ha! Ha! Ha!

When the princess Rosebud fell asleep, everyone in the palace fell asleep also and everything in the palace stopped. A great thorn hedge grew round the walls and, in time, completely covered the palace. Then, a hundred years later to the very day, the good fairy guided a horse, ridden by a gallant prince, to the palace.

Prince ✳ Whoa! Stand still a moment!
What is this green mountain which I see before me?

Good Fairy But is it a mountain? Are you sure?

Prince Hallo! Where are you?
I heard a voice and yet I cannot see anyone.

Good Fairy I am here, but you cannot see me.
Tell me, what can you see?

Prince I can see a great, green mountain … I think.
But I cannot be sure, because it is not made of grass. Instead, it
is full of sharp thorns.

Good Fairy Many princes have tried to get through those
sharp thorns and have been stabbed to death. Have you got
courage, young prince?

Prince I hope so. Yes, I think so.
I think I can say that I have got courage.

Good Fairy Good! Now, if I told you that the most beautiful
girl in the world lies sleeping beneath those cruel thorns, what
would you say?

Prince I would say that I would go to her.

Good Fairy Are you brave enough to risk your life amongst
those cruel, sharp thorns in order to rescue a girl you have never
seen?

Prince Yes, I am. I will go.

Good Fairy Wait! Close your eyes for ten seconds and then
open them again.

Prince   Ten seconds!
One ... two ... three ... four ... five ... six ... seven ... eight ...
nine ... ten!
Can I open them?
CAN I OPEN THEM?
The voice didn't answer.
Oh well, she did say open after ten, so I will.
Oh!
It must be some sort of magic!
All the sharp thorns have changed into beautiful rosebuds.

Good Fairy   I am still here. Leave your horse tied to the gate
and follow the sound of my voice.

Prince   ＊Whoa! Stay there, my good fellow.
It is just as I said before.
It is some kind of magic.
Now I am walking, but I do not know where I am going.

Good Fairy   Follow me! Follow me!

Prince   Who are you?
Please tell me that.

Good Fairy   I am the good fairy. You cannot see me and you
cannot touch me, but you can always hear me if you listen
carefully. I am never far away.

Prince   Where are we going?

Good Fairy   We are going up the steps of the great palace
where no one has walked for a hundred years.

Prince   The doorman is asleep.
The footman is asleep.
The bird is asleep in its golden cage.
The clock has stopped and it is covered in dust.
Even the flies are asleep.
I am in a place where everything sleeps.

Good Fairy   Follow me! Follow me!

Prince   I am following you.
But why are we going up this tiny stairway?
What can there be up here?

Good Fairy   You will see! You will see!
Now you must open that door by turning the rusty old key in the lock.

Prince   * I can't.
I can't turn it.
It's too stiff.

Good Fairy   Try again! Try again!

Prince   * I can't.
It is ... just ... too ... stiff.
Please use some more of your magic and open it for me.

Good Fairy   No! That will not do! You must try again, unless you want to give up the chance of seeing the most beautiful girl in the world.

Prince   I will never give up.
I will try again.
* Now ...
It's open!

Good Fairy   Shut your eyes …
Walk in …
Now … Open them …

Prince   Oh! I can't believe it?
A beautiful, sleeping princess!
You were quite right.
She is the most beautiful girl in the world.
What shall I do?
What shall I do *now*?
… She must have gone again.
But she did say that she was never far away.

Good Fairy   Good! I can see that you are
beginning to trust me.

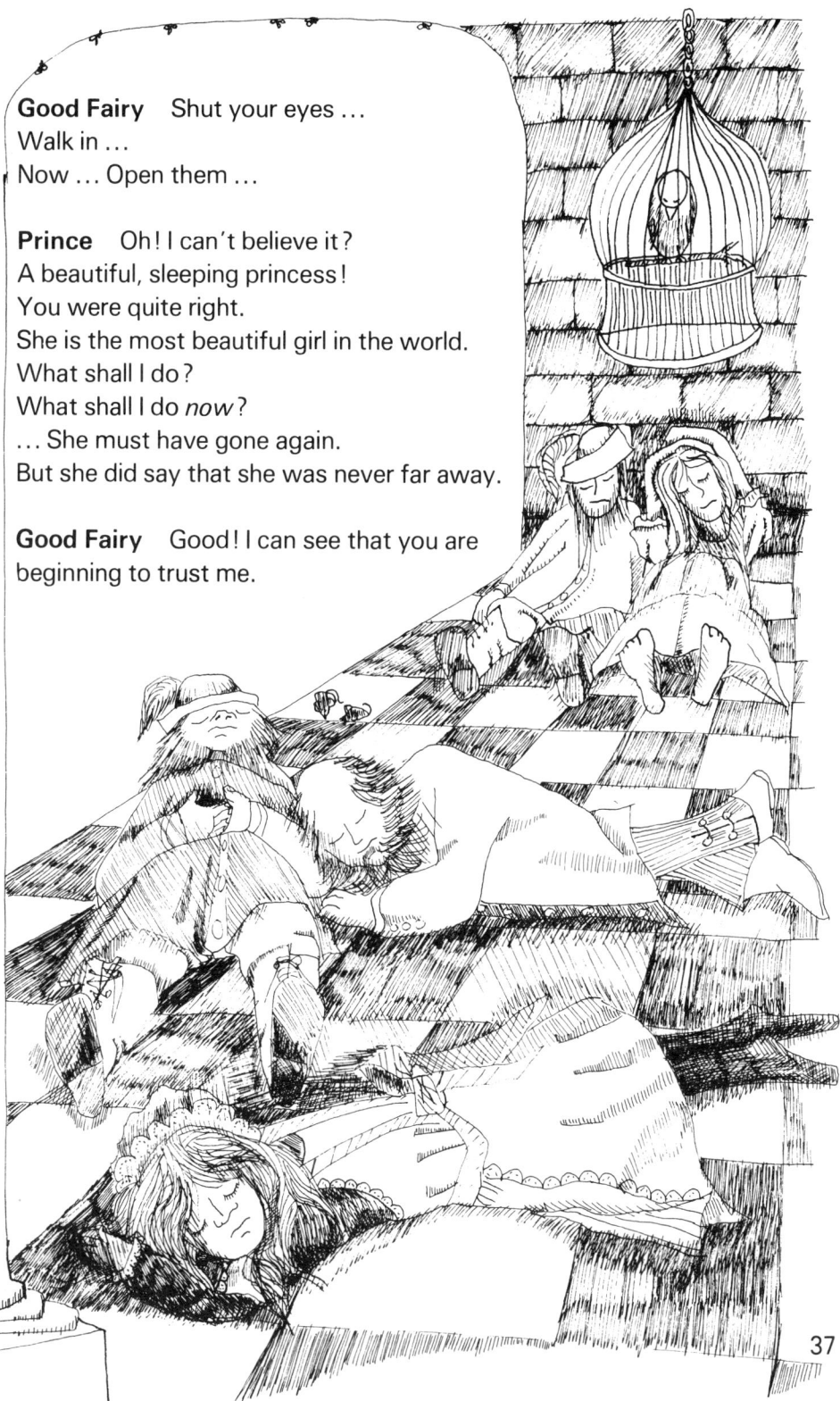

Prince   I'm glad you're back!
I want you to tell me what to do with this sleeping beauty now
that I have found her.

Good Fairy   You must decide that for yourself, for I am going
now.
Goodbye! G ... o ... o ... d ... b ... y ... e!

Prince   I am all alone with her.
She is like the rosebuds which grew on the thorns round the
palace.
Hallo, beautiful Rosebud.
I will give you a kiss. *
Oh! She is opening her eyes.
She is looking at me.
She is smiling and ...

When the prince kissed the princess the whole palace woke up
as if the hundred years of sleep had been but one second. The
prince and the princess were married and lived together happily
ever after.

Rumpelstiltskin

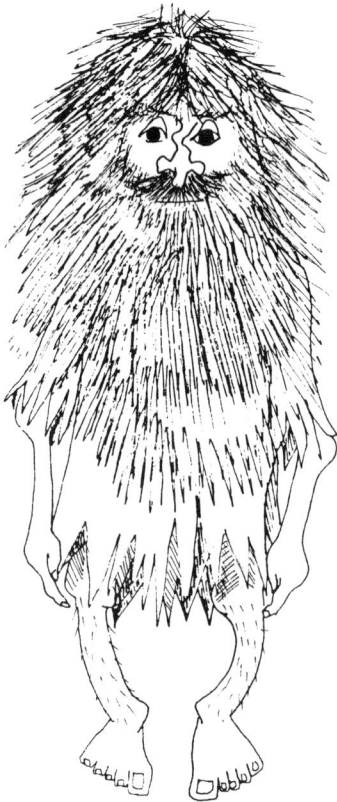

The people in the story are:

Rumpelstiltskin

Miller's Daughter

King

Messenger

A miller boasted to the king that his daughter could spin straw into gold. The king sent for the girl and put her in a room filled with straw. The king said that the miller's daughter would die if she did not spin the straw into gold before morning.

Miller's Daughter   I cannot do it. * Oh! Oh!
I know I cannot do it.
No one can spin straw into gold.
Oh, I wish I was back at home.
I wish ... I wish ... I wish ...
 * Oh! Who is that at the door?

Rumpelstiltskin   Good day to you.

Miller's Daughter   Who are you, little man? Are you a friend?

Rumpelstiltskin   Maybe I am! Maybe I'm not!
I might be your friend.
Tell me why you are crying.

Miller's Daughter   I'm crying because I must spin this straw into gold before morning. If I can't do it, the king says that I must die.

Rumpelstiltskin   What will you give me if I spin the straw into gold?

Miller's Daughter   I would give you anything in the world. But I am only a miller's daughter and I have so little to give. Will you take my necklace?

Rumpelstiltskin   That will do, miller's daughter. I will spin the straw into gold and you can give me your necklace when I am done.

Miller's Daughter   I will sit and watch while the wheel turns.

Rumpelstiltskin   * Spin away, spin away,
Lo and behold!
Spin away, spin away,
Straw into gold!

Miller's Daughter   Oh! You can do it. You can spin straw into gold. It's magic! How do you do it? Tell me your secret.

Rumpelstiltskin   No, that is my secret.

Miller's Daughter   Tell me how! Tell me how!

Rumpelstiltskin   No, that is my secret which can never be told.

Miller's Daughter   The reels are full of fine, gold thread. How pleased the king will be.

Rumpelstiltskin   You must give me your necklace, miller's daughter.

Miller's Daughter   I give it gladly. Now you must be gone, little man. * Go quickly, for I can hear footsteps.
 * Someone is knocking at the door.

43

Messenger   Good morning, miller's daughter. I have come to tell you that the king is on his way. Is your work done?

Miller's Daughter   Come in and see for yourself.

Messenger   Oh! So you *can* spin straw into gold. How pleased the king will be. This room is full of treasure.

Miller's Daughter   * Listen! Someone is knocking at the door.

Messenger   It is the king. Come in, your majesty. The miller's daughter has finished her work.

Miller's Daughter   Yes, come in and see, your majesty. Look! The room is full of fine, gold thread. You have a room full of treasure.

King   That is good.
That is very good.
Now I have gold.
I have a room full of gold.
But I must have more.

Miller's Daughter   No! No! Your majesty! You have so much gold already.

King   I must have more.

Miller's Daughter   But this room is full of gold.

Messenger   Shall I unlock the door to the next room, your majesty?

King   Yes, we will go to the next room. *

Miller's Daughter   Oh no! This room is even bigger than the last one and there is far more straw.
Please, your majesty! Don't lock me in here.

King   I will lock you away
for a night and a day.
Spin this straw into gold
Or you will grow cold.

Messenger   The king means that you must spin this straw into gold or you will die. We shall be back in the morning, miller's daughter, so do your work well.

Miller's Daughter   I cannot do it. * Oh! Oh! I know I cannot do it. I wish … I wish … I wish that funny little man would come back and help me.

Rumpelstiltskin   And here I am!
I see that you are crying again, miller's daughter.

Miller's Daughter   Oh, please help me again, little man. Help me like you did last time.

Rumpelstiltskin   What will you give me this time if I spin the straw into gold?

Miller's Daughter   I will give you the very last thing I have in the world. I will give you this little ring from my finger.

Rumpelstiltskin   That will do. I will spin the straw into gold and you can give me the little ring from your finger when I am done.

Miller's Daughter   I will sit and watch while the wheel turns.

Rumpelstiltskin * Spin away, spin away,
lo and behold!
Spin away, spin away,
Straw into gold!

Miller's Daughter Oh! You have done it again. It's magic!
Please tell me how you do it.
Please tell me the secret.

Rumpelstiltskin No. That is my secret.

Miller's Daughter Please! Please! Please!
Please tell me how.

Rumpelstiltskin No, that is my secret which can never be
told.

Miller's Daughter The reels are full of fine, gold thread again.
How pleased the king will be.

Rumpelstiltskin You must give me the little ring from your
finger, miller's daughter.

Miller's Daughter I give it gladly. Now you must be gone,
little man. * Go quickly, for I can hear footsteps.
* Someone is knocking at the door.

Messenger Good morning, miller's daughter. I have come to
tell you that the king is on his way. Is your work done?

Miller's Daughter Come in and see for yourself.

Messenger Oh! You have done it again. How pleased the king
will be.

Miller's Daughter Listen! * Someone is knocking at the door.

Messenger   It is the king. Come in, your majesty. The miller's daughter has finished her work.

Miller's Daughter   Yes, come in and see, your majesty. Look! Once again the room is full of fine, gold thread. You have another room full of treasure.

King   That is good.
Now I have more gold.
Now I have more treasure.
But I must have more and more.

Miller's Daughter   No! No!
Your majesty! You have two
rooms full of treasure already.
You cannot want more.

King   But I do.
I want more treasure.
I must have more treasure.

Messenger   Shall I unlock
the door to the next room, your majesty?

King   Yes, we will go to the next room. *

Miller's Daughter   Oh! Oh! This room is bigger than the other two put together. I have never seen so much straw. Please, your majesty, I cannot do it again. You don't understand.

King   Spin this straw into gold
as you have been told
and I'll make you my wife,
for the rest of your life.

Messenger   The king means that he will marry you if you spin this straw into gold. Do your work well, miller's daughter, and you will be queen.
We shall be back in the morning.

Miller's Daughter   Can the king really mean that he will marry me if I spin this straw into gold? Then I should be a queen. Oh, how I wish that I could do it and be the queen.
I wish … I wish … I wish …
If only that funny little man would come back …

Rumpelstiltskin   Here I am!
I see that you are not crying this time, miller's daughter.

Miller's Daughter   No, because the king has promised to marry me and then I shall be queen.

Rumpelstiltskin   Ah! But what has the king told you to do?

Miller's Daughter   I've got to … I mean you've got to …
I mean, *please* will you spin this straw into gold?

Rumpelstiltskin   But there is so much more straw this time.

Miller's Daughter   I know you can do it. Please help me just once more. Please help me to become queen.

Rumpelstiltskin   What will you give me if I help you to become queen?

Miller's Daughter   Alas! I have nothing left to give. But I can give you something after I have become the king's wife for then I shall be queen. I shall be rich.

Rumpelstiltskin   If I do it you must give me your first child when you become queen.

Miller's Daughter   I will! I will! I will give you anything if only I can become queen.

Rumpelstiltskin   Do you promise to give me your first child?

Miller's Daughter   I do! I do! I promise to give you my first child.

Rumpelstiltskin   Put your hand in mine and say, I PROMISE TO GIVE YOU MY FIRST CHILD.

Miller's Daughter   I PROMISE TO GIVE YOU MY FIRST CHILD.

Rumpelstiltskin   That will do.

Miller's Daughter   I will sit and watch while the wheel turns.

Rumpelstiltskin   * Spin away, spin away, lo and behold!
Spin away, spin away, straw into gold!

Miller's Daughter   Oh! You have done it again. It's magic!
Now I shall be queen. That's a kind of magic too.
Please tell me how you do it.
Please tell me how to spin straw into gold.

Rumpelstiltskin   No, that is my secret.

Miller's Daughter   You are a funny little man. Why! I don't even know your name. What *is* your name?

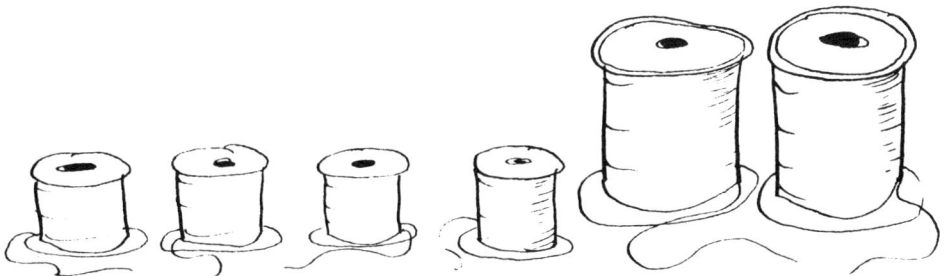

Miller's Daughter   Well, what do I care? Don't tell me then.
I don't care.

Rumpelstiltskin   Don't care was made to care.
So, miller's daughter … BEWARE!

Miller's Daughter   He's gone again. But I don't care because
this great room is full of fine, gold thread.
* Ah! I can hear footsteps. * Someone is knocking at the door.

Messenger   Good morning, miller's daughter. I have come to
tell you that the king is on his way. Is your work done?

Miller's Daughter   Come in and see for yourself.

Messenger   Oh! You have done it again. How pleased the king
will be.

Miller's Daughter   Listen!
* Someone is knocking at the door.

Messenger   It is the king.
Come in, your majesty.
The miller's daughter has finished her work.

King   Ah! That is good.
Now I have gold for the rest of my life.

Miller's Daughter   And please, your majesty, you promised
that I should be your wife.

King   You shall, my dear.
I have gold for the rest of my life,
and you, miller's daughter, shall be my wife.

And so it was that the miller's daughter married the king and
one year later a beautiful child was born.
Now it so happened that, one day, when the queen was sitting
alone, there came a knock at the door.

Miller's Daughter ✱ Come in, whoever you are!
Oh! It's you. It's the little man who can spin straw into gold. I
had forgotten about you.

Rumpelstiltskin But I have not forgotten about you, miller's
daughter.

Miller's Daughter I am no longer just a miller's daughter,
little man. I am the queen now and I no longer have to spin straw
into gold. Why have you come to see me?

Rumpelstiltskin I have come to see you because of the
promise you made.

Miller's Daughter What promise?

Rumpelstiltskin Have you forgotten the promise you made?

Miller's Daughter Yes, I have. What promise are you talking
about, little man?

Rumpelstiltskin You must *think*, miller's daughter.

Miller's Daughter You must not call me miller's daughter. I
am a queen now.

Rumpelstiltskin Yes, you are a queen and you have a child.

Miller's Daughter Oh yes! I *do* remember you. Of course I
remember you. I gave you my necklace and the little ring from
my finger.

Rumpelstiltskin You gave me your necklace for the first
room of gold.
You gave me the little ring from your finger for the second room
of gold. Now you will give me your ...

Miller's Daughter   No! No! Never!

Rumpelstiltskin   Then you *do* remember the promise you made.

Miller's Daughter   Go away, you wicked little man.

Rumpelstiltskin   Not until you give me your child.

Miller's Daughter   You know that I cannot do that. You know that I cannot give you my beautiful child. Listen! I will give you all the riches in the kingdom if you will go away and never come back.

Rumpelstiltskin   What are riches to me?
I can spin straw out of gold if I want to be rich.
I want something I can love. I want the child.

Miller's Daughter   No!
I will do anything else you ask, but I
will never give away my child.
Never! NEVER! N E V E R!
There must be something else.

Rumpelstiltskin   Maybe there is.
Maybe there isn't.
I know one thing you can do.
You can tell me my name.

Miller's Daughter   But I don't know your name. I remember you said that your name was another of your secrets which could never be told.

Rumpelstiltskin   I will give you three days.
If you can find out my name in three days, I will go away.
Then you can keep your child and you will never hear from me again.

Miller's Daughter   I will find out what your name is.
I promise!
Come back tomorrow and I will tell you what it is.

Rumpelstiltskin   I will do that.
Good day.

Miller's Daughter   Messenger! Messenger!

Messenger   Yes, your majesty?

Miller's Daughter   It is said by my husband, the king, that you are a very wise man. Now, tell me, do you know the name of every man in the kingdom?

Messenger   The names of all the men in the kingdom are written in *The Great Books of Names*, your majesty.

Miller's Daughter   Oh! That is wonderful! If all the names are written in a book, everything will be all right. Bring *The Books of Names* to me, Messenger.

Messenger   Do you wish me to bring, *The A, B, C, Book of ORDINARY Names* of all the people in the kingdom, and *The Great Book of EXTRAORDINARY Names*, your majesty?

Miller's Daughter   Yes, I will have both books. Tell me, is *every* name in these books.

Messenger   There are nine thousand, nine hundred and ninety-nine names in the books, your majesty, so … well … just one might be missing.

Miller's Daughter   Just one might be missing, you say. Then you must go and find it. Go to every house in the kingdom, but be back in two days' time.

Messenger   Very well, your majesty. I will do as you say.

Miller's Daughter   When that little man comes back, I will read every name in, *The A, B, C, Book of Ordinary Names*, to him. Let me see how it begins …
A is for Alan and Andrew and …
B is for Ben and Bob and …
C is for …
∗ Oh! Who is that at the door?

Rumpelstiltskin   It is …
Ah! But I must not tell you my name!
What is that book you are reading?

Miller's Daughter   It is *The A, B, C, Book of Ordinary Names* of all the people in the kingdom.

Rumpelstiltskin   Ask me one that begins with letter J.

Miller's Daughter   Letter J …
Is your name John?

Rumpelstiltskin   No, that's not my name.
Ask me one that begins with letter M.

Miller's Daughter   Letter M … Is your name Michael?

Rumpelstiltskin   No, that's not my name.
Ask me one that begins with letter W.

Miller's Daughter   Letter W … Is your name William?

Rumpelstiltskin   No, that's not my name. Ha! Ha! Ha!
You will never get it and I will tell you why.
It's not in the Book. Ha! Ha! Ha!
Good day! I'll see you tomorrow.

THE ABC BOOK OF ORDINARY NAMES

A is for:

Alan	Ann
Andrew	Alice
Adam	Anna

Miller's Daughter   Oh dear! Oh dear! What can I do?
What can I do to keep my beautiful child?
I know! I'll read all the names in the other Book. I didn't really
think that such a funny little man would have an ordinary name.
Now, let me see. All the names in this Book are very odd.
A is for Abracadabra. That isn't a name. It's a spell.
B is for Bandy-Legs. I'm sure that's what his name is. I'm sure
… I'm sure … that's … what … his … name … is … Oh! I'm so
sleepy, but … I'm … sure … that's … what … his … name … is.

Rumpelstiltskin   What *is* it then?

Miller's Daughter   Oh! You did give me a start! Will you
please knock on the door before you come into the room?

Rumpelstiltskin   I will when I come back tomorrow.

Miller's Daughter   Ah! But you won't need to come back
tomorrow because I've found out what your name is.

Rumpelstiltskin   Tell it to me then.

Miller's Daughter   Promise me that you will go away and
never come back. Promise me that I can keep my child.

Rumpelstiltskin   Only if you can tell me my name.

Miller's Daughter   All right! It's Bandy-Legs.

Rumpelstiltskin   No! That's not my name. Ask me another.

Miller's Daughter   Oh dear! It must be another one beginning
with B. It's Bully-bags.

Rumpelstiltskin   No, that's not my name. Ask me another.

THE BOOK of EXTRAORDINARY NAMES

A

is for:

Abracadabra
Apple pan dowdy
Annagamoochi
Alabulla

Miller's Daughter   Oh please, give me a clue. Please! Please!

Rumpelstiltskin   Just open the Book and tell me the letter on the page.

Miller's Daughter   All right!
It's letter ... N.
I've got it! I've got it! It's Nobble-Nose!

Rumpelstiltskin   No, that's not my name. Ha! Ha! Ha!
You will never get it and I'll tell you why.
It's not in the Book! Ha! Ha! Ha! I'll see you tomorrow.

Miller's Daughter   What shall I do? Oh, what shall I do? He says that his name isn't in *The Ordinary Book of Names*, or in *The Book of Extraordinary Names*, Oh! I'm so unhappy. Oh! I wish I had never become queen. I wish I had never had my beautiful child.
Why doesn't the messenger come back?
I shall just cry myself to sleep until morning ... Oh! ... Oh! ... Oh! ...

Messenger   Your majesty! Your majesty! Wake up!

Miller's Daughter   Oh! It is morning! Tell me the name!
Quickly! Tell me the name!

Messenger   I have been to every house in the kingdom, but I have not been able to find a missing name.

Miller's Daughter   Then you haven't looked properly. You lazy ... idle ... good-for-nothing ...

Messenger   No! No! Your majesty, do not be angry, because I have a tale to tell.

Miller's Daughter   But have you found the missing name?

Messenger   I have not been able to find a single missing name, but late last night, as I came to a high mountain at the end of the forest, I saw a little house. Now, outside this house a fire was burning and round about the fire a strange little man was dancing.

Miller's Daughter   Oh, what was he like? Did he have a funny nobble-nose and bandy-legs?

Messenger   Yes, yes, your majesty.

Miller's Daughter   But did he tell you his name?

Messenger   Well … no … he didn't exactly *tell* me his name.

Miller's Daughter   Then you don't know it. Why do you play tricks on me? You are a …

Messenger   I beg you to listen to the rest of my tale, your majesty.
Now, as I watched, this little fellow danced about on one leg, and shouted: 'Today I'll brew and then I'll bake.
Tomorrow I shall the queen's child take.
How lucky it is that nobody knows my name is RUMPEL-STILT-SKIN!'

Miller's Daughter   Rumpelstiltskin! That's it! That is his name.
Oh how happy I am again, for now I shall be able to keep my …
Messenger, you can go, but you shall be rewarded. *
Now I can keep my beautiful child for ever.
Listen! That is the sound of Rumpelstiltskin's footsteps. I'll sit here and wait for his knock. * Come in!

Rumpelstiltskin   Is the child ready for me, lady queen?

Miller's Daugher   Not yet. First I must have one more chance to tell you your name.

Rumpelstiltskin   You can have a hundred chances. You will *never* get it.

Miller's Daughter   I can try.

Rumpelstiltskin   What is the name then?

Miller's Daughter   Is your name Conrad?

Rumpelstiltskin   No, that's not my name.
Ha! Ha! No, that's not my name.

Miller's Daughter   Perhaps your name is ... Nicholas?

Rumpelstiltskin   No, that's not my name.
Ha, ha! Ha, ha!
No, that's not my name.

Miller's Daughter   Maybe ... maybe ...
your name is RUMPEL ... STILT-SKIN!

Rumpelstiltskin   Some witch has told you that!
Some witch has told you that!
* Ow! Ow! My foot!

Miller's Daughter   Ha, ha, Rumpelstiltskin, now you are in
such a rage that your foot has gone right through the floor.
Ha, ha! * Pull and tug, Rumpelstiltskin! Pull and tug!
* Oh! It's out and you've fallen right over!
Ha, ha! Ha, ha!

So Rumpelstiltskin went hobbling off as best he could and he
was never heard of again.